Egg Holders

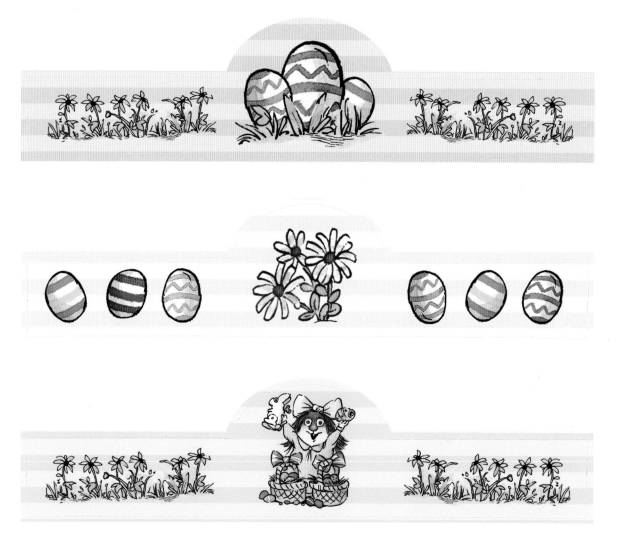

1. Carefully press out each egg holder.
2. With each one, form a ring around an egg to get the correct size, and tape the ends together.
3. Place your decorated Easter eggs in the rings!

HAPPY EASTER, LITTLE CRITTER®

BY
MERCER MAYER

**For Tanya
and Dustin**

A Random House PICTUREBACK® Book

Random House 🏠 New York

Happy Easter, Little Critter book, characters, text, and images copyright © 1988 Mercer Mayer
Little Critter, Mercer Mayer's Little Critter, and Mercer Mayer's Little Critter and Logo are registered trademarks
of Orchard House Licensing Company. All rights reserved. Published in the United States by Random House Children's Books,
a division of Penguin Random House LLC, 1745 Broadway, New York, NY 10019, and in Canada by Penguin Random House
Canada Limited, Toronto. Originally published in slightly different form by Golden Books, an imprint of Random House
Children's Books, New York, in 1988. Pictureback, Random House, and the Random House colophon are registered trademarks of
Penguin Random House LLC.

Visit us on the Web! • rhcbooks.com • littlecritter.com

ISBN 978-1-9848-5158-1

MANUFACTURED IN CHINA

10 9 8 7 6 5 4

Random House Children's Books supports the First Amendment and celebrates the right to read.

It's Easter morning.
I bet the Easter Bunny
has already come.

I'll quietly tiptoe downstairs . . .

and find all the Easter goodies
before anyone else wakes up.

But, as usual, my little sister
is up before me.

I got a toy egg that you can look into, a wind-up bunny, some candy chickens, a bunch of chocolate eggs, and millions of jelly beans.

The Easter Bunny gave my little sister the same things.

Dad says that's so we won't argue.

Mom says we can't eat any of it
until after breakfast.

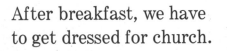

After breakfast, we have
to get dressed for church.

Dad starts the car, and we all get in.

My little sister likes to get all dressed up, but I don't.

At church, I can't see anything because
everyone is wearing funny hats.

After church, all the kids
dye Easter eggs.

I think my eggs are the best.

While the eggs dry we have a big picnic lunch.

Then our parents hide the eggs in the field. We're not supposed to peek.

Next, we all line up . . .

and run into the field to find the eggs.

Sometimes too many kids find the same egg.

Sometimes you walk right by an egg,
and someone else finds it.

Sometimes the little kids don't find any,
so you have to help them.

But by the time we go home, everyone has had a happy Easter.

Egg Holders

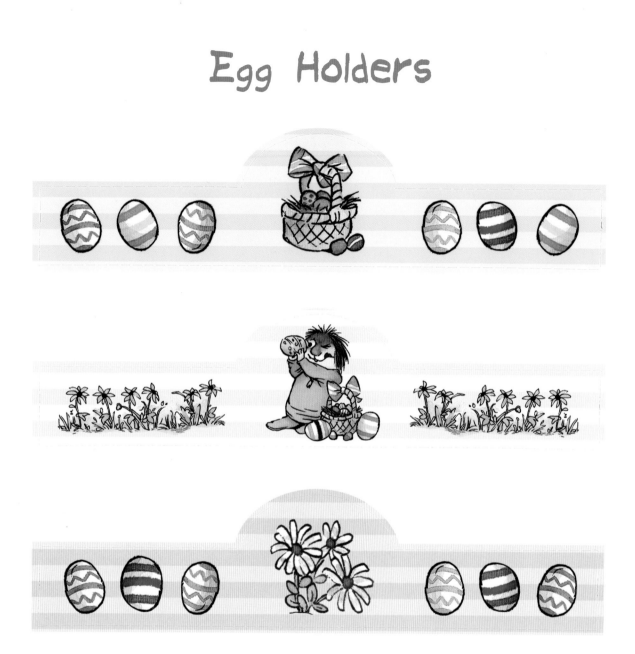

1. Carefully press out each egg holder.
2. With each one, form a ring around an egg to get the correct size, and tape the ends together.
3. Place your decorated Easter eggs in the rings!